# The Light in
# Bradford Manor

## The Gun Lake Adventure Series
## Book 6

by Johnnie Tuitel and Sharon Lamson

**Cedar Tree Publishing**

THE LIGHT IN BRADFORD MANOR
Copyright 2004 by Johnnie Tuitel and Sharon E. Lamson

Published by          Cedar Tree Publishing
                      1916 Breton Road, SE
                      Grand Rapids, MI 49506
                      1-888-302-7463 (toll free)
                      www.tapshoe.com

**Cedar Tree Publishing**

Cover and Illustration: Dan Sharp

Library of Congress Catalog-in-Publication Data
Lamson, Sharon E. 1948-
Tuitel, Johnnie, 1963-

cm.—(The Gun Lake Adventure Series)

Summary: Johnnie and his friends spend two weeks at Indiana's Camp Riley—a camp for children both with and without disabilities. Camp life proves to be more than campfires, ghost stories and activities. Johnnie meets his first girlfriend, wrestles with some jealousy, conquers some fears and finds himself inside a real ghost story.

ISBN 0-9658075-5-X

[1. Adventure stories—Fiction 2. Mystery and detective stories—Fiction 3. Physically Handicapped—Children—Fiction 4. Indiana—Fiction

I. Title    V. Series: Lamson Sharon E. 1948-, Tuitel, Johnnie, 1963

(the Gun Lake Adventure Series)

"What if they got caught?" Nick whispered.

"If they got caught, we can only hope they don't squeal on us," said Travis in a low voice.

Before Johnnie could say anything, he heard a crunching noise on the path behind him. A few seconds later, Katy, Robyn and Charlie appeared.

"Whew!" said Robyn. "I'm glad you guys are here. This is the scariest adventure we've ever been on."

"What? You're afraid of ghosts?" asked Joey.

"No! I'm afraid of getting caught by our counselors," she replied.

The clear, moonlit sky made traveling down the road easy. No one said a thing as they moved along. It took about ten minutes to reach the bottom of the road. Straight ahead and up the driveway stood the manor. The moonlight reflected off the roof and white trim. Crickets sang in the night. Katy suddenly looked up and gasped.

"What's the matter?" Danny asked.

"What are those things flying around?" she asked.

Johnnie looked up. Against the night sky, he could see what looked like black birds darting back and forth. "Bats," he said.

"Bats!" Katy's voice rose to a high-pitched whisper.

Danny grabbed for her arm. "Don't scream," he cautioned. "They are just looking for insects. They won't bother us."

"L-look!" Charlie pointed toward the manor.

A dim, glimmering light shone from the kitchen window. Just then, someone's silhouette by the kitchen window, and then disappeared.

"Do you think whoever that was saw us?" Johnnie's voice shook. "Quick! Hide in the shadows."

"The shadows are creepy," Katy whined.

"It's creepier out here in the open where we can be seen," Danny said. "Come on! Let's go!"

They scampered to a huge bushy tree at the bottom of the hill.

"Shh!" Travis warned. "Listen."

Johnnie held his breath. He heard his heart thudding in his chest. But aside from that and the night crickets, everything was quiet. Deadly quiet.

Johnnie let his breath out slowly. "We have to get closer," he said.

"I don't want to get closer," Katy whispered.

"Well, we can't see anything from down here," Johnnie whispered back. "I say we go for that big maple everyone to see. "It's a speaker!"

"Hmm. No wires," said Nick. "Must be one of those wireless speakers."

Everyone stared at Nick and rolled their eyes.

"Ya think?" Travis joked. "Nick, ace detective figures out that a wireless speaker doesn't have wires."

"Ha, ha," Nick said. "Very funny."

Johnnie interrupted them and said, "You know, my guess is there's another speaker in the cellar."

Robyn looked around. "Hey, guys!" she said. "Did you notice how quiet it is? No wind. No rain. No crickets. Something doesn't seem right."

"The storm stopped, and you think something's not right?" asked Katy.

"It does seem kind of spooky," Charlie said.

Suddenly, a large gust of cold wind took them by surprise. It seemed to come out of nowhere. A loud blast of the siren made them all jump.

"Oh no!" Johnnie cried. "Tornado!"

Everybody but Johnnie and Charlie scurried down the cellar steps.

"Hey!" Johnnie yelled. "What about us?"

The siren drowned out his voice. Panic set in. Johnnie saw Charlie push her chair closer to the cellar steps. Surely, she wasn't thinking of rolling down the steps?

Abandoned! His friends had abandoned him in their own panic. And now Johnnie was left outside to face the tornado alone.

"I guess I'll have to fall out of this stupid wheelchair and try scooting down the steps," he cried.

Just then, above the sound of the siren and the ever-increasing roar of the wind, Johnnie heard someone yell his name.

He looked toward the driveway. Someone was running toward him. A big flashlight beam bobbed up and down as the person ran.

Johnnie froze. What should he do? Yell? Try to hide? What?

Charlie, who had stopped at the opening of the cellar, made the decision for him.

She flicked on her light and screamed, "Over here!"

Within seconds, PJ joined them on the porch. "What are you doing here?" he demanded.

The siren wailed again. "Never mind that now," PJ said. "We need shelter—*now!*

"The cellar door's open," Charlie shouted.

He grabbed Charlie and hoisted her down the steps. He called back to Johnnie, "Don't worry! You're next!"

Within seconds, PJ reappeared on the porch and lifted Johnnie out of his chair. The roar of the wind barreled down on them like a freight train. Johnnie felt the wind pull at him as he and PJ struggled toward the cellar. PJ pushed Johnnie onto the cool cement floor and handed him his flashlight.

"Keep the light on me so I can close and latch the cellar door," he yelled. PJ bolted back up the steps. Johnnie watched as he struggled to close the door. The wind practically ripped it out of his hand.

Travis ran up the steps to help him. Between the two of them, they closed the door and secured the latch. The wind roared and howled like an angry animal,

PJ and Travis scrambled down the steps.

"Everybody, back!" PJ shouted. "Get as far back into the cellar as possible." The light from his flashlight reflected dismally off the gray-colored cement floor and walls.

Johnnie breathed heavily as he scooted toward the back. He bumped up against Danny, shined his flashlight in his face and said, "Thanks for leaving me and Charlie on the porch. I thought was going to die up there!"

Danny's mouth dropped open. He placed his hand on Johnnie's shoulder and said, "Oh, my gosh! I am so sorry. I was so scared I wasn't thinking about you. I'm really sorry, Johnnie."

Johnnie felt the surge of anger begin to leave him, but he felt shaky inside. "It's OK, I guess. I mean, I am alive—thanks to PJ!"

Feeling suddenly tired, Johnnie leaned back against the wall. To his amazement, he nearly fell back into a hole in the wall. "Hey! What's this?" he yelled.

PJ aimed the light where Johnnie sat. His eyes opened in surprise. "Looks like someone's been digging," he shouted.

Curiosity overtook Johnnie's fear and anger. He flashed his light into the cavernous hole. The darkness made him feel uneasy, so he scooted away from the hole. He decided to wait out the storm before doing any more exploring.

The wind howled, and the cellar door rattled. Suddenly, he became aware that Charlie had crawled over to sit beside him. He could feel her trembling.

"Are we going to make it?" she asked in a small voice.

Johnnie tried to make his shaky voice sound as brave as he could. "Yeah. We'll be fine. You'll see."

"Hey! I think the storm is passing," Robyn said.

"I can still see lightning and hear thunder," Katy said.

"Yeah, but the thunder is moving away, and the wind has died down," Robyn insisted. "I bet we'll hear an all-clear siren pretty soon."

Robyn proved to be right—and Johnnie was never so glad that she was. The wind departed, the thunder and lightning moved on to wherever they were going. Johnnie heard the gentle steady rain against the closed cellar door.

PJ climbed the stairs and unlatched the door. He pushed against it until it opened. Johnnie saw him shine his light around outdoors. Then PJ came back down into the cellar.

"That was close!" he said. The tornado definitely touched down. There are tree limbs, small trees and junk all over the lawn."

"That was a tornado?" yelled Johnnie. "We were in a real tornado?"

PJ frowned. "Yes, and all of you could have been killed. I want to know what you kids were doing out here."

"Don't you want to know what that hole in the cellar wall is all about?" Johnnie asked.

PJ sat on the floor and planted his flashlight on the floor so the beam hit the ceiling. "All in good time, Johnnie," he said. "First, I want to know what's going on, and I want to know *now*."

CHAPTER 13

# Gold Digger

The kids fumbled over their words as they tried to explain why they were at the manor. Johnnie knew they were all in big trouble, but he hoped PJ would somehow understand.

"You saw a ghost. You heard a ghost. You saw a muddy footprint. And then the cellar door was unlocked and open. You risked your lives for an adventure. Not only that, you sneaked out of the cabin. If anything had happened to any of you, Camp Riley would have been held responsible." PJ looked intently at each of the campers.

He sucked in a large breath of air and exhaled loudly. "Well, while we're down here, let's investigate that hole in the wall. But *I'm* going to do it, and then we're all going back up that hill to the cabins."

Johnnie scooted to one side as PJ shined the light

into the hole. He reached in and pulled something out. A speaker.

"So, this is how your ghost let his or her voice be heard," PJ said. "Pretty high-tech for a ghost."

"Hey!" a hoarse voice yelled down into the cellar. "Who's down there?"

PJ scrambled away from the hole and shined his flashlight up into the angry face of Pierre. "It's just me and some of the campers. We had to take shelter down here when the tornado hit."

"Well, it's over now. You'd best get out of there," he snarled.

PJ led the way for the others to follow. He carried Charlie out with him and said he'd be back for Johnnie. While Johnnie awaited his turn, he turned on his own flashlight and shined it into the hole. It went back farther than his light would shine. So, this is where the muddy footprint came from, Johnnie reasoned.

PJ reappeared in the cellar and lifted Johnnie up over his shoulder. "Amazingly, your wheelchair and Charlie's weren't damaged. They're still sitting on the porch."

As they moved down the driveway, Johnnie looked up at the manor. He caught his breath. "Look!"

he cried. "There's someone in the kitchen."

PJ and the others stared at the window. Sure enough, a figure of a woman walked past the window. A dim light flickered from within.

Pierre came around the side of the house and demanded to know what they were still doing there. "Listen, we're on our way," said PJ. "It's not like you own this house, or anything. We just saw someone in the window and wondered who it was."

Pierre's eyes popped open, and he scurried down the driveway without looking back.

"That was strange," PJ said. "Wait here. And I do mean, *wait here.*"

He jogged around to the back of the house. Johnnie could hear him bang on the back door and yell, "Is anybody in there?"

Johnnie kept his eye on the kitchen window. The light became dimmer and eventually went out. A moment later, PJ reappeared.

He said, "The backdoor is locked. If someone's in there, he or she doesn't want to answer the door. Let's get back to the cabins. I'll talk to Carol about it tomorrow."

\*     \*     \*

When Johnnie and his friends arrived back at the cabin, Phillip, Tom and the other campers met them at the door. "Where were you guys?" Phillip cried. "When the siren went off and PJ and you boys were gone, we were worried."

PJ did his best to explain what had happened. Phillip and Tom were clearly upset. Johnnie thought for sure they'd all get another lecture. He could only imagine what the girls were going through. At least he and the guys had PJ to speak for them.

The next morning, Travis, Danny, Joey, Nick and Johnnie met in Carol's office, along with Charlie, Robyn and Katy. PJ went with them. Johnnie's mouth felt dry, and his palms were sweaty. He cringed at what Carol would probably say to them.

Carol sat behind her desk until every camper was in her office. Her face looked pale and her eyes were red, like she'd been crying. Slowly, she stood behind her desk. Johnnie noticed her hands shake. Suddenly, he felt awful. He was sorry he and his friends had caused everyone so much worry.

Carol took a deep breath and looked at the kids sitting before her. "I am so sorry," she began. "I had no idea that by trying to protect the camp I would have put you kids in such danger."

Johnnie's eyes widened in surprise. What was she talking about?

"I had information given to me that said someone was looking for the gold bricks that were supposedly buried on the property. The people who gave that information to me are very reliable and trustworthy. I noticed footprints on the porch and traced them into the woods behind the manor.

"Remember the story I told about the maid and how she had fooled some other gold diggers into believing there was a ghost on the property? Well, I rigged up some wireless speakers, dressed in a maid's uniform and used a nightlight to light up the kitchen just enough so whoever was out there would see my silhouette. I had a wireless microphone and cried out, 'Go away,' in as ghostly a voice as I could come up with."

She sat back in her chair and shook her head. "At first, it seemed to work. I saw someone run away from the manor and into the woods. But apparently, the person wasn't convinced. I saw more footprints. The night of the storm, I left for the manor to check on everything. The cellar door was wide open, and I heard someone shuffling around. I had my microphone with me, and I screeched, 'Go-o-o awa-a-ay,' as loudly as I could. I had no idea my voice would carry all the way up to the amphitheater."

Johnnie's mouth quivered. He saw Robyn hastily wipe tears from her face. "We're sorry, Carol," he said. "We got caught up in the adventure of discovering a real ghost, and didn't think about any danger."

Carol tried to smile. "I don't know who is trying to find gold here. There isn't any. The Bradfords used to mine sand on this land. The sand was transported to a company in Indianapolis where they made bricks. The family business earned a lot of money. Someone once said the Bradfords' bricks turned into gold. I'm guessing that's where the rumor started."

PJ scratched his chin thoughtfully. "I think I know who has been digging," he said.

Carol looked at him in surprise.

"When we were all huddled in the cellar, Pierre the chef seemed pretty upset that we were there," PJ continued. "On our way down the driveway, we saw you in the window—only, of course, we didn't know it was you. He saw you too, and suddenly he was in a hurry to get out of there."

"Plus," Johnnie added, "there is a hole in the wall

that leads into a kind of tunnel."

Carol nodded. "I know," she said. "I discovered that recently and planted the speaker there. Hmm. That would explain why Pierre always insisted on doing his baking at the manor. He said his French pastries would bake better in the manor's oven. PJ, would you go find Pierre? I have a few questions to ask him."

She stopped a moment and then added, "By the way, that was quite the storm, last night. I'm glad I made it back here before it hit.

Johnnie felt a chill creep up his spine. If Carol had made it back before the tornado, then who was the woman in the window?

\*    \*    \*

At lunchtime, Carol and PJ joined Johnnie and his friends at their meeting table. "We thought you'd like to know about Pierre," Carol said. "As it turns out, he really is a chef who specializes in French cooking. But his real name isn't Pierre. It's George Rex—a distant relative of the Bradfords. He had heard the rumor about the gold bricks and figured he'd dig it up for himself. He thought the money should 'stay in the family,' as he put it."

"That's amazing!" Charlie said. "Did he get

arrested?"

"No. We did ask him to leave and not come back. I think he's convinced the gold bricks don't exist. We did tell him that if he ever came back, we'd have him arrested for trespassing," said Carol.

"Now, as for you guys," PJ said. "We called your parents and told them everything. The bad news is, they were really upset and wanted to come down early and take you home. The good news is, we talked them out of it. We said we'd make sure you didn't escape again. And we also promised them you'd do some kitchen duty—especially since Pierre's gone."

"We have to cook?" Katy said. "The only thing I can make is cereal with milk on it."

"No, you don't have to cook," Carol said. "The counselors and I will take turns with meals. But you can help clean up garbage, rinse dishes, wipe tables, sweep floors…"

"We get the picture," Johnnie said. "Actually, that does seem fair."

"Good!" said PJ. "You can start right now. If you all work together, you can join us down at the Universal High Course when you're through."

\*   \*   \*

The rest of the week went by quickly. When it was time for the parents to come, Johnnie wished he could spend another week there—without kitchen duty. He watched as Travis and Charlie laughed and kidded around with each other. He still felt that twinge of jealousy.

When Charlie's parents came to pick her up, she wheeled over to Johnnie. He was surprised when he saw tears in her eyes. "We have each other's email addresses," she said. "Please write to me. I'm really going to miss you."

"More than you're going to miss Travis?"

Charlie looked surprised. "I like Travis," she said, "but not the same way I like you. Write to me, okay?"

Johnnie smiled and held her hand. "You know I will. And next summer, we'll have another great adventure!"

Charlie laughed. "Maybe we'll find out who was really in the window that night."

She wheeled back over to her parents and let them help her into their van. As they pulled away from the campsite, she waved from the open window and blew Johnnie a kiss.

Johnnie's heart fluttered.

Just then Travis walked up to him. "Charlie's cool. PJ told me to find one other person to hang with who had a disability—and I did. I guess you and Charlie are OK. But I don't know about the rest of these campers."

He shrugged and walked over to say goodbye to PJ. Johnnie just shook his head.

\* \* \*

Finally, the van was loaded, and Johnnie and his friends were on their way home. Johnnie glanced out the window as they passed the manor.

Danny suddenly pointed toward the kitchen windows. "Look!" he said.

Johnnie pressed his nose to the glass. Was someone standing in the window? It looked like a woman wearing a maid's uniform. Was it someone who worked there? It seemed to Johnnie that she waved at them—but it could have been just a reflection off the glass.

Oh yeah. Next summer, they'd definitely have to come back to Camp Riley, Bradford Manor—and Charlie!

# Alternatives in Motion

A portion of the proceeds from sales of The Gun Lake Adventure Series goes to support the nonprofit organization Alternatives in Motion, founded by Johnnie Tuitel in 1995. The mission of Alternatives in Motion is to provide wheelchairs to individuals who do not qualify for other assistance and who could not obtain such equipment without financial aid.

If you would like to help out and make a donation, please send a check made out to Alternatives in Motion to the address below.

For further information please see our website or contact Johnnie Tuitel at Alternatives in Motion. Please call if you would like to arrange to have Johnnie Tuitel speak at your event or school.

Alternatives in Motion
1916 Breton Road SE
Grand Rapids, MI 49506
616.493.2620 (voice)
616.493.2621 (fax)
877.468.9335 (voice toll free)
www.alternativesinmotion.org

Alternatives in Motion is a nonprofit 501(c) (3) organization

**From Fox Lake Press, Chicago**

"Teaching your children about disabilities just got easier thanks to The Gun Lake Adventure Series."

**From the Children's Bookwatch—Midwest Book Review:**

"...A pure delight for young readers, *Discovery on Blackbird Island* is the third volume in "The Gun Lake Adventure Series," and like its predecessors, *The Barn at Gun Lake* and *Mystery Explosion!,* showcases the substantial storytelling talents of Johnnie Tuitel and Sharon Lamson.

"The fourth in Cedar Tree Publishing's outstanding "Gun Lake Adventure" series, *Searching the Noonday Trail* is another great novel by Johnnie Tuitel and Sharon Lamson for young readers which is wonderfully written and totally entertaining from first page to last."

"A most enjoyable and entertaining story, *Adventure in the Bear Tooth Mountains* is a welcome and commended addition to school and community libraries."

**From Reading Today:**

"What sets this apart is a character who is physically challenged … he does everything his cohorts do, only differently."

**From Early On Michigan Newsletter:**
    "This little book is a gem."

**From Pooh's Corner Bookstore:**
    "The Gun Lake Adventure Series provides action, adventure, fun and friends...elements kids love to read about."

**From the Grand Rapids Press:**
    "...(the) Gun Lake Adventure Series is capturing the attention of young readers in Grand Rapids and beyond."

**From the Statesman Journal, Salem, OR:**
    "A fine series for all children, who can have the fun of an adventure while learning that "different" doesn't mean inferior or threatening."

**From WE Magazine:**
    "An excellent venture."

## The Gun Lake Adventure Series
## by Johnnie Tuitel and Sharon Lamson

**The Barn at Gun Lake** (1998, Cedar Tree Publishing, $5.99 paperback, **Book 1**)
The Gun Lake kids stumble upon some modern pirates when they find an illegal copy of popular CDs in a deserted barn. While solving the mystery, there is a boat chase and then a dangerous wheelchair chase through the woods.

**Mystery Explosion!** (1999, Cedar Tree Publishing, $5.99 paperback, **Book 2**)
First there is an explosion. Then an arrest is made that shocks the quiet town of Gun Lake. A stranger in town and a search for his identity paves the way for another fast-paced mystery. Friendship and loyalties are tested as Johnnie Jacobson and his friends try to find the answers to "Who did it?" and "Why?"

**Discovery on Blackbird Island** (2000, Cedar Tree Publishing, $5.99 paperback, **Book 3**)
Blackbird Island is a small, quiet uninhabited island in Gun Lake. Or is it? A disturbing discovery sends Johnnie Jacobson and his friends on yet another Gun Lake adventure filled with schemes, action and mysteries to solve.

**Searching the Noonday Trail** (2000, Cedar Tree Publishing, $5.99 paperback, **Book 4)**
Summer's over and Johnnie is nervous about going to a new school. Will it be as adventuresome is the summer was? Johnnie's not too sure. But a secret football play and a field trip to where Chief Noonday and the Ottawa tribe used to live put Johnnie and his Gun Lake friends hot on the trail of another exciting adventure.

**Adventure in the Bear Tooth Mountains** (2003, Cedar Tree Publishing, $5.99 paperback, **Book 5)** A three-family Christmas vacation to the Bear Tooth Mountains in Montana test Johnnie and his friends' survival skills. Ghost towns, an mysterious old man, a blizzard and a mountain lion pave the road to challenges and daring.